Franny K. Stein

MAD SCIENTIST

MOOD SCIENCE

READ ALL OF FRANNY'S ADVENTURES

Franny K. Stein
MAD SCIENTIST

MOOD SCIENCE

JIM BENTON

SIMON & SCHUSTER BOOKS FOR YOUNG READERS

NEW YORK LONDON TORONTO SYDNEY NEW DELHI

SIMON & SCHUSTER BOOKS FOR YOUNG READERS
An imprint of Simon & Schuster Children's Publishing Division
1230 Avenue of the Americas, New York, New York 10020

SIMON & SCHUSTER BOOKS FOR YOUNG READERS
and related marks are trademarks of Simon & Schuster, Inc.
For information about special discounts for bulk purchases, please contact Simon & Schuster Special Sales at 1-866-506-1949 or business@simonandschuster.com.
The Simon & Schuster Speakers Bureau can bring authors to your live event. For more information or to book an event, contact the Simon & Schuster Speakers Bureau at 1-866-248-3049 or visit our website at www.simonspeakers.com.
Interior design by Tom Daly
The text for this book was set in Neue Captain Kidd Lowercase.
The illustrations for this book were rendered in pen, ink, and watercolor.
Manufactured in the United States of America
0721 FFG
First Edition
2 4 6 8 10 9 7 5 3 1
CIP data for this book is available from the Library of Congress.
ISBN 9781534413436
ISBN 9781534413450 (ebook)

For the librarians

CONTENTS

Franny K. Stein
MAD SCIENTIST

MOOD SCIENCE

CHAPTER ONE
FRANNY'S HOUSE

The Stein family lived in the pretty pink house with the lovely purple shutters down at the end of Daffodil Street. Everything about the house was bright and cheery.

And even though it was bright and cheery, Franny thought that if you just mixed the purple and pink paint together, you could paint the house much faster and then get on to more important things than the color of a house.

Many of Franny's recent inventions were all about mixing things together.

She'd gotten the idea the last time she saw her grandma, Granny Franny.

"Each of the individual things I put in my soup are good," she told Franny. "But when they're all mixed together, they somehow make it better."

"I wonder what kind of science is at work here," Franny said, holding up her grandmother to stir the pot.

"I also wonder how you keep getting smaller every time I see you, Granny Fran. I bet that in a couple years you'll be able to take a bath in a spoon," Franny joked.

"You might be right, Franny," Granny Franny said, chuckling. "But just because something is small, that doesn't mean it can't have a huge effect. Have you ever been bitten by a mosquito?"

Franny laughed.

"I get the point," she said.

"And thanks for teaching me how to make soup! I can't wait to get back to my lab and make my own version of soup."

Of course, Franny's Lab wasn't a pure Lab. He was also part poodle, part Chihuahua, part beagle, part spaniel, part shepherd, and part some kind of weaselly thing that wasn't even exactly a dog.

His name was Igor, and he was always ready to help Franny with her experiments....

Except when he was busy with his own stuff.

CHAPTER TWO
PUTTING THE PIECES TOGETHER

Maybe because Igor was a mix of so many different animals, he had a lot of different interests.

He liked cake decorating and karate and banana wrestling, which might sound easy, but Franny had accidentally created a pretty fierce banana, and it was Igor's job to play with it so it didn't become bored and start getting into trouble.

Igor's newest hobby was jigsaw puzzles, which took a long time for him to complete, since his little fingers were kind of stubby and plump.

Franny had no interest in solving a puzzle that others had solved before, so Igor put them together by himself.

This was fine with Franny because it allowed her to work on her experiments without Igor's help, and sometimes no help was exactly what she was in the mood for.

Franny was especially excited about her newest invention, the Mixer-Upper Machine. She'd gotten the idea from Granny Franny's soup.

"I made it with parts from a broken blender and an old nuclear reactor I had lying around. With it, I can combine good stuff to make something even better."

For one of her first Mixer-Upper experiments, she put a substitute teacher in it with a ruler. The machine made a whirring sound like a blender, and then it dinged like a microwave.

When Franny opened the door, the substitute teacher and the ruler had combined to make a foot-long sub.

It flopped around on the plate and threatened to make Franny stay after school unless she separated them again.

"Fine," Franny said. "I'll unmix you. But you might be making a mistake. Not everybody likes substitute teachers, but everybody can appreciate a delicious foot-long sub."

"Change me back!" the sub yelled.

"Okay, okay," Franny said, making some adjustments on the machine.

"You know, the other teachers warned me about helping you with your experiments. I should have listened to them!" the sub shouted.

"Perfectly understandable; everybody knows you should listen to the teachers," Franny said.

The next day she mixed an ice cream cone with a poodle and got a chili dog.

"I need to adjust this thing. I mean, I get it, but that's not even how you spell 'chilly.'"

Franny stayed up for the next two nights figuring out how to mix a duck with a beaver.

"This will be my greatest achievement yet!" she howled as she led them into her machine and explained it to them.

"All this device does is chop your molecules into chunks and then join those chunks together in a way that you two could never understand," Franny said with a pleasant smile.

"So just sit back, relax, and get chunked."

The machine made its familiar blender sound and then dinged.

The door opened, and Franny's newest creation stepped out.

"*A platypus?*" Franny shouted. "I can't believe I wasted all that time and all I got was a platypus! We already have those! We have a ton of those. This is nothing new!"

Franny lost her temper. She pounded on her machine and sent laboratory equipment flying.

She threw a wrench, which broke open jars from earlier experiments.

She kicked the table where Igor was just about to put the very last piece in the puzzle he had been working on for weeks.

She could tell he was upset, but she didn't care.

"Don't even start complaining about it!" she yelled. "It's just a dumb puzzle. It's not like the big important science experiments I do. You already knew how it was going to look when it was complete! The picture is right there on the box!"

Igor looked at all the pieces scattered on the floor. He had worked so long on that puzzle.

He opened his hand and let the last piece fall to the ground.

He walked away, and Franny saw a tear trailing down his face.

"Oh, it's just a silly puzzle!" she shouted at him. "A big waste of time!"

She stomped on the pieces.

"I probably saved you a lot of worthless effort," she shouted.

"That was pretty mean," the platypus said.

"You be quiet, beaver-duck," Franny snapped. "I can unmix you anytime I want."

CHAPTER THREE

I'LL BET THE PEPPERONI BUTTONS ARE GOOD

A couple of days had passed, and Franny hadn't been able to think of anything except how mean she had been to Igor.

She remembered how Igor had always supported her experiments, even when he didn't really think they were a good idea.

She thought back about how earlier that week he had helped out when she tried to develop a virus that would make people feel good all the time, instead of bad.

"I mean, think about it. Why do viruses always have to be bad? Smiles are contagious. Laughter is contagious. People should be able to catch all sorts of good things."

Igor nodded in agreement, even though he had no idea what he was agreeing to.

She remembered how, a few days before that, he had assisted her when she tried to develop a breed of attractive and wart-free toads so that people would want them as pets.

"Personally, I kind of like warts," Franny said. "But not everybody does.

"And toads would be great for people to have around. They eat bugs that bother us, like flies and mosquitos. And you know those can get in anywhere!"

She thought back to when he had helped her attempt to make clothes out of pizza so that when they got dirty, you could just eat them instead of having to wash them.

Actually, Igor thought this one was a terrific idea. From time to time he enjoyed eating nonpizza clothes, especially socks.

"He's always been a great assistant to me," Franny said. "I should have been nicer.

"I have to make this up to him. I'll do something silly to make him laugh," she said, and she got to work right away.

It didn't take her very long to finish his gift.

"He's going to love this!" she shouted, and ran to find him.

"Look, Igor! I wanted to apologize, so I made this for you!"

Igor just stared at it.

"It's a jigsaw puzzle with only two pieces! That way, you won't have to waste a lot of time putting the dumb thing together! Isn't that fun?"

Igor didn't think it was fun at all.

All it did was remind him of how long he had worked on the last puzzle before Franny wrecked it.

He walked away, leaving Franny holding the pieces.

"Fine!" she said. "I tried to apologize and you wouldn't accept it. Now it's your fault."

She stormed off and sat down at her work-bench.

She fiddled around with little bits of wire and gears, hoping to get her mind off what she had done, but Franny still felt terrible.

"I'm afraid I've hurt his feelings so bad that he'll never forgive me," she said quietly.

The platypus wanted to agree with her on this, but he knew it wouldn't go well if he did.

CHAPTER FOUR
IT'S NOT YOU.
IT'S ME.

Franny paced back and forth. She had a long list of things she wanted to work on, but she kept thinking about Igor.

First she'd get angry with herself, and then she'd come up with some silly solution, and then she'd get angry again, and then she'd start to worry about her projects.

"How could one little experiment cause all this trouble?" she asked, pulling on her pigtails.

"I've created much bigger problems than this before!" she shouted. "And none of them made me feel this way."

"Wait a second," Franny said, a thin grin crawling across her face.

"The problem here isn't what I *did*. The problem is how I *feel* about it. I can't work when I'm in one of these moods."

She looked over at her Mixer-Upper Machine.

"A little adjustment here and there, and I should be able to unmix *anything*."

The platypus hid under a table.

"I'm not unmixing you," Franny said, and a bolt of lightning cracked outside.

"I'm unmixing *me*."

CHAPTER FIVE
GETTING YOUR FEELINGS OUT IN THE OPEN

Franny finished some calculations and stepped into the Mixer-Upper.

"Phew! It still smells like a sub in here," she said. "I should install a fan."

She pressed a button and closed the door.

The machine whirred and dinged.

The door slowly opened.

Franny stepped out.

"Did it work?" she asked as she looked back into the machine.

"C'mon out!" she shouted. "Come out here."

Four figures stepped out. They looked somewhat familiar.

They looked a little bit like ... Franny.

"What dumb idea have you had now?" the angry-looking Franny snarled.

"It's simple. You're my feelings and I've removed you. You were getting in the way," Franny said. "Now maybe I can get something done."

Angry-Fran kicked a piece of lab equipment and grumbled.

"I could have figured that out myself," she snapped.

Franny stepped up to a frightened-looking version of herself.

"Do you know who *you* are?" Franny said.

"I'm afraid to ask," the other Franny said.

"That's right!" Franny said. "You are afraid. You're my fear. You're Scaredy-Fran."

Scaredy-Fran gasped. "Yikes!"

"I know which feeling I am," another one of the Franny look-alikes giggled. "I'm Elephant-Fran."

"An elephant is not something you feel," Angry-Fran snapped.

"Oh no? I'll bet if an elephant sat on you, you'd feel it," the other Franny said, and then she laughed and laughed.

"I can see that you're my silliness," Franny said. "You're Silly-Fran."

"And you want to . . . get rid of us?" the last Fran asked, with tears welling up in her eyes.

"That's right, Sad-Fran," Franny said. "You feelings are just getting in my way. Everything goes wrong when I start feeling too much."

"You're so dumb," Angry-Fran said. "You have more than four moods. We're not the only feelings in there."

"I know that there are more than four feelings," Franny said calmly. "I'll do the rest later. I wasn't even sure that this would work."

She pointed at the platypus. "I mean, take a look at that thing. This is new technology."

The platypus frowned.

Franny closed the door on the Mixer-Upper and went to look over her list of projects.

"Wait a second. What are *we* supposed to do?" Scaredy-Fran whimpered.

"You're *feelings*, right?" Franny asked them. "So go do whatever you *feel* like."

The feelings looked around the lab. They had never been on their own before.

Franny waved her arms. "C'mon, Scaredy-Fran, Silly-Fran. You're moods, aren't you? I've heard of something called mood swings. Maybe you could go find some of those to play on."

"I guess I could go find something to get mad about," Angry-Fran sneered.

"And I'm sure I can find something miserable to enjoy," Sad-Fran said, sighing

"Yes, you can all go find things that interest you," Franny said impatiently.

"When should we be back?" Scaredy-Fran whined.

"I don't think I'll *ever* need you back, so how does *never-o'clock* sound? Just stay out of my way and stay out of trouble. I have a whole long list of projects I can finally complete without you pests slowing me down."

And with that, her feelings went off to do whatever they felt.

"I mean, most animals don't live in houses with people. What's the big deal if a few more leave home?"

Without her feeling of sadness, the project just didn't seem very important to her, and she crossed it out.

CHAPTER SIX

JUST NOT FEELING IT

Franny looked through her long list of projects.

"Here's one that I wanted to get started on—inventing an ice cream that would never melt."

Franny thought for a moment.

"I must have been feeling pretty silly when I thought of that," she said. "Ice cream that never melts? Isn't that just a *milk-shake?*"

Without her silly side, Franny didn't feel like pursuing that one, and she crossed out the idea.

"Okay, let's have a look at the next one," she said, reading down her list.

"A robot that finds your lost pet because it's so sad when somebody loses a pet.

"I don't know. When I think about it now, that doesn't really seem that sad to me."

She looked out the window.

"Look. There's that weird toad I created hopping away, and I really don't care.

She looked at the next project on her list.

"Ah!" she said with a smile. "Now, *this* one should be good. It has a monster in it. I always enjoy making monsters."

Her notes described making a giant, slobbery creature that would sit on the roof of your house.

"Oh, yes, and it has *slobber*. This has real potential," Franny said.

She kept reading her notes. They said that if your house caught on fire, the monster would drool all over it and put out the fire.

"I like the drooly part," Franny said, "but what does a house fire have to do with it?"

She read the note she had written on the sketch. It said, *FIRES ARE SCARY*.

"Your house catching on fire is supposed to be scary?" Franny scoffed. "That doesn't scare me."

Without her fearful side, Franny didn't see the point in pursuing it.

That was the last thing on her list. She had no more projects written down.

"No more projects to do?" Franny asked. "That used to really upset me."

She climbed down from her chair and shuffled over to a couch, where Igor was watching TV.

"But I got rid of my angry side. So I really don't feel mad that I have nothing to do.

YAWWNNN

"In fact, I really don't feel like doing any-thing."

And she plopped down next to Igor and stared at the TV....

For a very long time.

CHAPTER SEVEN

I'VE NEVER NOT FELT LIKE THIS BEFORE

Igor wasn't upset with Franny anymore, and he really liked watching TV with her. But after a couple of days of watching TV, he began to notice that Franny didn't laugh at the funny parts. She didn't get sad when tragic things happened.

When they watched a scary movie, Franny never screamed or jumped.

Sometimes Igor would pick a really bad movie just to see if Franny would get angry about it.

But Franny never reacted very much at all. Without her feelings, she was kind of boring.

Igor had seen Franny be a lot of things, but never boring.

Eventually they didn't watch anything but the news.

CHAPTER EIGHT

DUTY CALLS

"This just in," the newscaster on the TV said. "Reports are coming in that a strange new disease is turning people into toads."

Igor sat up straight and stared at the TV. Franny just shrugged. She didn't feel anything.

"Meh," she said. "It's probably my fault."

"Scientists have shared this sketch," the newscaster said. "They believe that the illness may have started with this toad, which seems to have been infected with a highly contagious virus."

Igor recognized it as the toad Franny had created. He ran to look in the bowl where she'd kept it. She had broken the bowl during her tantrum, along with the test tube that had held her virus.

"Yes, Igor," she said with a yawn. "I'm way ahead of you. That escaped toad of mine must have caught that virus I created and it mutated. I've probably accidentally released a horrible thing into the world. I suppose it's going to end pretty badly.

Franny took the remote from Igor's wet, warty green hand.

"What's the deal with your hand?" she asked. "You should probably switch to a different soap."

But it wasn't the soap. Igor had caught the disease. He, too, was beginning to transform.

"Igor, don't take this the wrong way," Franny said, "but EWW."

"Sometimes I wonder if leaving weird viruses just lying around might not be a good idea."

Igor held up the broken bowl the toad had been kept in.

"Look lots of things I make can be an eensy-weensy bit life-threatening. That's just the way it is."

The TV began to show scary pictures of people turning into toads.

"See? You see there?" she said, pointing weakly at the screen. "They look just like my toad. Yes, this is *definitely* my fault."

But Franny wasn't scared.

The TV showed pictures of people crying about their families turning into toads.

But Franny wasn't sad.

And when the reporter said that th[e] ness was "toadly awful," she didn't lau[gh].

Franny wasn't silly anymore.

"Igor, hand me the remote," she said

Franny got up from the couch and hopped over to her refrigerator.

"That's weird," Franny said. "When did I start hopping?"

A fly went past, and for just a moment Franny thought about snatching it out of the air with her tongue.

"I guess I'm turning into a toad too," she said, and shrugged. "Just like the rest of the world."

Igor stared at her with big, terrified eyes, which were beginning to look a bit toady.

"Oh well," she said. "That's how it goes sometimes, with these worldwide toad diseases."

"Oh, no it's not!" a little voice called out. "That's NOT how it goes."

Franny looked around.

"Where is that voice coming from?" she asked.

"I'm in here," the voice said.

"Somebody is in the Mixer-Upper," Franny said, and she opened the door.

A small, determined-looking version of Franny stepped out.

"How did you get in there?" Franny asked.

"Angry-Fran *told* you there were more than four feelings. I was still in there, but you shut the door on me."

"Why didn't you say something sooner?"

"I'm pretty quiet until I have a reason to speak up."

"Who are you?" Franny asked.

"I'm your sense of duty," she said.

"Did you say *'doody'*?" Franny asked. "Because *if* I still had a silly side, I might laugh at that."

"Not 'DOODY.' I'm your sense of DUTY.
It's spelled d-u-t-y. I'm the feeling you have
when you know that you just have to do
something, even if you don't really feel like
doing it."

"I don't really feel much of anything,"
Franny said.

"Well, I do," Duty-Fran said forcefully.
"And I'm afraid we don't have much time."

"You're kind of pushy," Franny said.

"Well, yes. That's kind of my whole thing," Duty-Fran said. "Let's go."

"Where are we going?" Franny asked.

"We're getting all your parts back together," Duty-Fran said. "You might say that we're going to *herd your feelings.*"

Duty-Fran grinned broadly at Franny, who looked back at her with no expression.

"Your silly side would have thought that was *funny,*" Duty-Fran said.

CHAPTER NINE

KEEPING YOUR FEELINGS TO YOURSELF

Franny put some horrifying traps and chains on the table.

"What are these for?" Duty-Fran asked.

"To catch them," Franny said, adding a strange device to the pile. "This is a paralyzing ray. After I blast them, we can stick them in this bag."

"No, no, no," Duty-Fran said, shaking her head. "I'm afraid your lack of feelings has made you a little heartless. We can just talk to them."

"I have a device you can strap onto your mouth that will make your voice painful to listen to when you talk. Will that help?" Franny asked.

"Maybe some other time," Duty-Fran said. "For now we'll just talk regularly."

As they headed outside, they passed a toad hopping around in the kitchen.

"I guess that's my mom," Franny said. "I'll bet that's why nobody stopped me from watching TV all week."

"What?" Duty-Fran cried. "YOUR MOM? That's terrible!"

"I'll have to take your word for that,"
Franny said. "Because I'm really not feelin' it."

"We have to hurry!" Duty-Fran said, pulling Franny along by the wrist.

They soon found Angry-Fran out behind the garage, breaking bottles.

They watched as she picked one up, smashed it, and then yelled at it for breaking so easily.

"You deserve to be broken!," she yelled at it. "I wish I had broken you a long time ago."

Duty-Fran stepped up.

"We need you to come with us," she said.

"Forget it. I like being out here on my own, expressing my feelings—I only have the one, but I like to express it."

"Okay," Duty-Fran said. "We wouldn't want to make you mad." And they started to walk away.

"Wait. I don't mind being mad," Angry-Fran growled.

"Yes, of course, but this is the type of thing that will really make you lose it."

"I'm all about losing it," Angry-Fran said. "You wouldn't believe the things I can lose it over. One time I couldn't find my gum, and I went NUTS. Over gum!"

"Fine," Duty-Fran said. "Follow us."

"The next feeling might be harder to find," Duty-Fran whispered to Franny. "They won't all be as loud as bottle-smasher here."

"Do we really have to do this?" Franny groaned. "When you think about it, *not* doing things is so much easier. And it's faster, too."

"We must do what we must do," Duty-Fran said.

Soon they found Sad-Fran in the yard behind some bushes. She was blowing bubbles and crying when they popped.

"I never really got to know that bubble," she sobbed. "It was over so quick."

"Did you see some puppy toys out here?" Duty-Fran asked her.

"Puppy toys? No. Why?"

"We have a bunch of tiny, chubby puppies that have lost their favorite toys," Franny said, immediately understanding what Duty-Fran was planning.

"They must be miserable!" Sad-Fran said hopefully.

"Might be the saddest thing I ever saw," Duty-Fran said. "And they're pretty chubby. Well, we'll see you later."

They began to walk away when Sad-Fran trotted up next to them.

"Could I see the puppies?" she asked.

"They're too sad," Franny said.

"And chubby," Duty-Fran added.

"Well, actually," Sad-Fran began, "I really feel my best when I feel my worst."

"If you must," Duty-Fran said. "But you'll probably cry your eyes out."

"I can't wait!" Sad-Fran said as she clapped her hands and bounced along behind them.

"These two were easy," Duty-Fran whispered to Franny. "But I have no idea how we're going to get Silly-Fran to come along. This could take some time."

"I think I know," Franny said.

They found Silly-Fran under a tree by the side of the house.

"What are you doing?" Duty-Fran asked her.

"I'm digging a hole," Silly-Fran said.

"What for?" Franny asked.

"Holes are good for keeping stuff in," Silly-Fran said.

"Like what?" they asked her.

"Well, for starters, I'm going to need a place to put all this dirt I dug up," Silly-Fran said. "And I think it's going to fit perfectly in there."

Franny handed her a doughnut.

"I need you to put this on your head," Franny said. "Stick out your tongue and follow us, but walk backward."

"That makes total sense to me," Silly-Fran said, and off they went.

"How did you know what to do?" Duty-Fran asked her.

"I just used the only thing that made sense," Franny whispered. "*Nonsense*."

"I'm glad to see that you're feeling ready to get to work on this," Duty-Fran said.

"I don't really feel anything at all," Franny said. "I just want to be done so I can go lie down and become a toad."

Duty-Fran scowled. "Only one more to go," she said, and she noticed that Franny was starting to look a bit more toadish. "And there's not much time."

"Scaredy-Fran should be easy," Franny said.

"Don't be so sure. Fear is often the hardest feeling to overcome," Duty-Fran said.

CHAPTER TEN
NOTHING TO FEAR BUT FEAR ITSELF, WHICH, LET'S BE REAL, IS PRETTY SCARY

They looked everywhere for Scaredy-Fran and couldn't find her.

"She's hiding," Duty-Fran said. "And we're running out of time. Can that dog of yours sniff her out? Dogs can smell fear."

"He seems to be mostly toad now," Franny said. "And you know he was never really *all* dog to begin with. He's part Lab, part poodle, part Chihuahua, part—"

"Yes, yes, a weaselly thing," Angry-Fran interrupted. "We've heard this a jillion times."

"So what do you suggest we do?" Duty-Fran asked.

"I've given that a lot of thought," Franny said. "I think the best thing we could do is — *just give up.* I mean, maybe it will be okay to be a toad."

Duty-Fran gasped.

"You're just saying that because you're missing some important feelings. Normally, this would make you mad, or sad, or scared."

"You're right," Franny said. "And it's a good thing I got rid of those dumb things."

"NO! Everybody needs feelings. They are troubling at times, but without them, people are a bunch of . . . toads, I guess—just sitting there staring blankly, not doing much of anything.

"And that's going to make things very difficult when the ghosts arrive."

"What ghosts?" Franny asked.

"The ghosts," Duty-Fran said. "Yeah, they show up every time something like this happens."

"What are you talking about?" Franny asked.

Duty-Fran raised her voice a bit. "THE GHOSTS. They always show up about now."

Franny scoffed. "I'm not afraid of ghosts, you know. I mean, I was when I was little, but not anymore."

"That's because you don't have a sense of fear. But I know somebody who does."

Scaredy-Fran burst out from her hiding place in the closet.

"No! Not ghosts! Save me! Save meeeeeee!!!" she screamed.

"Come with us," Duty-Fran said. "We know where you'll be safe."

Scaredy-Fran cuddled up next to them. "Okay. Let's go," she whimpered.

CHAPTER ELEVEN
JUST PULL YOUR-SELF TOGETHER

Back in Franny's lab, Duty-Fran was taking charge.

"Okay, Angry-Fran, get in the machine."

"I thought you said you were going to show me something to make me mad," Angry-Fran growled.

"You're right. I did. But I was lying to you. I'll bet that makes you mad."

"SO MAD!" Angry-Fran shouted. "AND I REALLY APPRECIATE THAT!" And with a sneer, she walked into the Mixer-Upper.

"You're next," she said to Silly-Fran. "But you don't need to go in there."

"Why not?" Silly-Fran giggled.

"Because you're already in there," Duty-Fran said.

"No I'm not."

"Check it out if you don't believe me," Duty-Fran said, and Silly-Fran walked in to take a look.

"Well? Are you in there?" Duty-Fran yelled into the machine.

"I sure am," Silly-Fran said. "I guess you were right."

"Hey," Franny said. "You sure picked up that silly stuff quickly."

"Duty makes you rise to the occasion, Franny. It makes you do things you didn't know you could."

Franny coughed.

"Oh no," Duty-Fran said. "Are you feeling okay?"

COUGH COUGH COUGH

"A slight cough. Nothing to worry about,"
Franny said. "Just a little frog in my throat."

"A little more than just your throat,"
Duty-Fran said. "And look at your dog."

Franny was transforming quickly, and Igor was almost all toad.

"Not much time left," Duty-Fran said.

She grabbed Sad-Fran by the hand and led her to the machine. "I know I told you there would be puppies, but there aren't."

A tear rolled down Sad-Fran's face.

"Are you disappointed?"

"Very," Sad-Fran sobbed.

"Disappointment is a lot like sadness, right?"

"It's close enough," Sad-Fran sighed. "Thank you." And she walked in.

"You might not want to watch this," Duty-Fran said to Franny. "It's not going to be very nice."

"What are you going to do?"

Duty-Fran walked right up to Scaredy-Fran and pushed in close to her.

"I have something to show you, Scaredy-Fran."

"Is it a spider or something like that? I'm not afraid of those."

"Oh, it's much scarier than that."

"Like a monster?" Scaredy-Fran said. "I like monsters."

"We grew up together. I know exactly what you like," Duty-Fran said, her voice falling to a low, threatening growl. "And I know what scares you too."

"You do? Okay. Let's see what you have."

"I'm going to show you. But first take this."

She handed Scaredy-Fran a broom.

"A broom? Why would I be scared of a broom?"

"Because we told Mom that you'd clean your room, and she's on her way up the stairs now."

"There's not enough time! Why would you tell her that? She's going to be so mad!"

Scaredy-Fran jumped into the Mixer-Upper and trembled in the dark. Mom was pretty scary when you lied to her.

"You know who's next, right?" Duty-Fran asked.

"You mean us,?" Franny asked, her voice a little toadier than before. "I was thinking about that."

Duty-Fran crossed her arms. "What were you thinking?"

"I'm still not convinced I need those other feelings," Franny said. "You and I can do everything by ourselves. Just brains and duty. Let's ditch the other feelings."

An old lady's voice spoke from the corner, "That's not going to work."

It was Franny's grandma.

"Granny Fran! How long have you been here?"

"Long enough to hear all I needed to," she said. "It sounds like I didn't do a very good job teaching you about soup."

"What does this have to do with soup?" Franny asked.

"Each ingredient makes it better. You're like a pot of soup. You need all of your ingredients."

"But isn't the soup good even if it's missing one or two ingredients?" Franny asked. "It doesn't need every single little thing, does it?"

"Maybe not," Granny Fran said, "but why wouldn't you want to make the best soup you could?"

"Let's look at it another way," Duty-Fran said. "Think about puzzles like the ones Igor does."

"They're a waste of time," Franny scoffed.

"Puzzles are complicated, and so are people. Both are made up of lots of little parts."

"What's your point?"

"My point is that if you want to see the whole picture, you need to put all those little parts together," Duty-Fran said.

Franny thought about it.

"Yeah, I don't know if that makes sense...."

"SO JUST HURRY UP AND HOP INTO THE GIZMO, TOAD GIRL, BEFORE IT'S TOO LATE!" Granny Fran shouted.

Franny smiled.

"I never knew my granny and my sense of duty were so much alike," she said. "Okay, I'll do it."

Franny tapped a few buttons, and she and Duty-Fran walked into the machine and shut the door.

"It's too dark in here," Scaredy-Fran whimpered.

"Not for long," Franny said.

The machine started up and whirred. It dinged like a microwave, and out stepped Franny, all in one piece, but still looking pretty toady.

She hopped to her lab table. She was afraid that maybe she was too late to stop the toad virus, and she felt pretty silly for how she had acted.

She felt sad that so many people had suffered, and angry with herself for letting it all happen.

"Hey," she said. "I think I have all my feelings back.

"And it's up to me to fix this," she added, smiling when she recognized her sense of duty shining through her other feelings.

"You know, I think my sense of duty might be my favorite one of all."

CHAPTER TWELVE

PUTTING BUGS INTO THE SYSTEM

Franny's fingers became so stubby and toady that it was hard for her to finish her work on the vaccine, but she didn't give up, and she finally completed it just before she totally transformed.

"Toadly," she chuckled to herself. Her silliness was definitely back.

She used it on herself first, and it worked perfectly. She cured Igor next.

"Granny Fran, I'd give you a dose of medicine, but you look fine to me."

"It's probably because of all that homemade soup I eat," Granny Fran said with a grin.

"How will I ever get this medicine to everybody? That's, like, eight billion shots!"

The number was terrifying.

She felt overwhelmed.

"I hate this!" she shouted. "I hate these feelings!"

Granny Fran patted her gently on the back. "Our feelings are what make us move forward—they inspire us."

"But this is a HUGE problem, Granny Fran. I'm not big enough to handle this."

"You remember what we talked about at my house the other day?"

"I sure do. It was something . . . something . . . soup, I think."

"That's right. But we also talked about how small things can have a big effect. Just because you're small doesn't mean you can't solve this."

"You've just given me an idea!" Franny said. "It's a little silly, but it might work."

Franny opened a window.

"Bugs are attracted to you, Igor. Just sit here by the window for a minute."

It wasn't long before a mosquito flew in, and Franny captured it in a jar. Then she took it and a needle full of the medicine and put them together in the Mixer-Upper.

After the machine had done its blending, Franny proudly showed Granny Fran and Igor the results.

"It's a mosquito, but when it bites you, it injects you with the cure. I'll make a whole bunch of these and then just turn them loose."

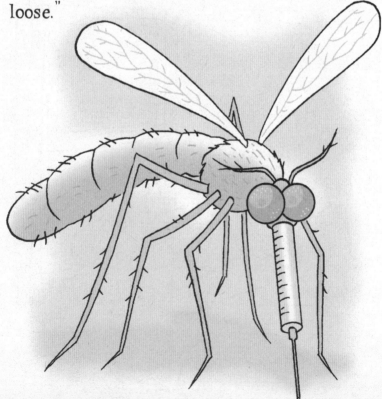

"Won't the toad people just eat the mosquitos?" Granny Fran asked.

"Even if they do, they'll still get the medicine. I developed it so that it would work either way.

"And mosquitos have a way of getting in everywhere. Before you know it, everybody will be cured."

"But how will you make enough of them?" Granny Fran asked.

"Just stick it in the copier and turn the dial to eight billion. My gosh, Granny, haven't you ever seen a copier before?"

CHAPTER 13
A MILE IN YOUR SHOES

In a matter of weeks, the medicated mosquitos managed to get everywhere, and pretty soon everybody had recovered and things went back to normal.

"I don't think I want to do any more mixing for a while," Franny said. "But before I take this thing apart, I'd like to try one last mix."

The Mixer-Upper whirred for a moment then and made the ding sound like a microwave oven.

There was a hiss and the door opened, and a very strange figure stepped out.

It was Franny and Igor, *mixed together.*

Their two bodies were mixed together, but so were their two minds.

They could hear through each other's ears, see through each other's eyes.

"WOW. This fur is really itchy. I can't believe that you ever stop scratching yourself!"

After walking around for only a few minutes, they were ready to be unmixed. They hit a few buttons and stepped back into the machine.

"I'll bust that thing up later," she said. "I get why you like puzzles now. It feels good to work on a problem that you KNOW can be solved. Can I do one with you?"

Igor smiled and made room for her at the table.

"I wanted to apologize, so I made you a special puzzle," Franny said.

There was a whirr and a ding, and the door creaked open again.

Franny gave Igor a big hug and said "Why don't you go play or something while I take this thing apart?"

Franny watched as he got out one of his puzzles and made space on the table to put it together.

She felt like she understood him better, after being all mixed up with him for a minute.

She set down her wrench and joined him.

"I used a painting you made of us together. It's pretty much my favorite painting in the whole world."

The two worked on the new puzzle for hours and hours.

Even Franny's mom, who was no longer a toad, sat down and helped.

After that, Franny always tried to appreciate and respect Igor's interests. Having your molecules chopped into chunks with somebody will do that.

Although she never really got why he liked eating socks.

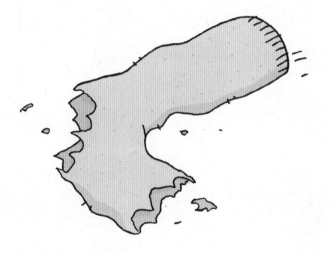

Jim Benton

is a *New York Times* bestselling writer and cartoonist whose unique brand of humor has been seen on toys, television, T-shirts, greeting cards, and even underwear. Franny K. Stein is the first character he's created especially for young children. A husband and father of two, he lives in Michigan, where he works in a studio that really and truly does have creepy stuff in it.